TOM'S FISH

NANCY COFFELT

TOM'S FISH

NANCY COFFELT

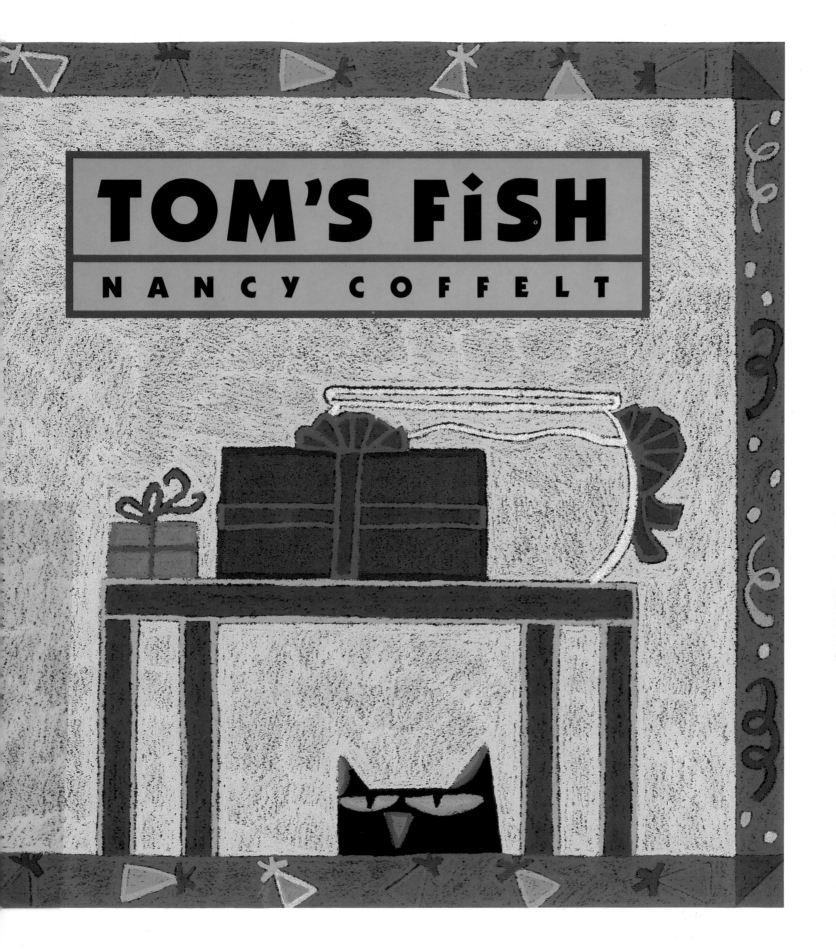

GULLIVER BOOKS

HARCOURT BRACE & COMPANY

San Diego   New York   London

Printed in Singapore

Library of Congress Cataloging-in-Publication Data
Coffelt, Nancy.
Tom's fish/Nancy Coffelt.—1st. ed.
p. cm.
"Gulliver books."
Summary: Tom tries to stop his goldfish from swimming upside
down, until he finds a way to appreciate his pet's individuality.
ISBN 0-15-200587-0
[1. Fishes—Fiction. 2. Individuality—fiction.] I. Title.
PZ7.C658To 1994 [E]—dc20 92-44114

First edition A B C D E

For Sarah Soyster,
who made me think of it,
and for Liz Van Doren,
who made it happen

The illustrations in this book were done
in Caran D'ache oil pastels on black Canson paper.
The text type was set in Meridien
and the display type was set in ITC Kabel Ultra
by Harcourt Brace & Company Photocomposition Center,
San Diego, California.
Color separations by Bright Arts, Ltd., Hong Kong
Printed and bound by Tien Wah Press, Singapore
Production supervision by Warren Wallerstein
and David Hough
Designed by Camilla Filancia

On his birthday, Tom got some great presents. He got a magnifying glass, a dinosaur puzzle, and a new bike.

But his favorite present was a goldfish.

His very own goldfish. A shiny orange fish in a shiny
glass bowl full of clear water all the way to the top.

Tom named him Jesse.

But Tom noticed something very odd about his goldfish.
Tom's goldfish swam upside down.

Tom turned the bowl this way. Tom turned the bowl that way. Jesse stayed upside down.

"He needs a view," said his sister. So Tom put Jesse's bowl on the windowsill where he could see outside.

Jesse swam around in circles but stayed upside down.

"Maybe he's bored," said Tom's father.
Tom drew a picture of a clown fish for Jesse.

It didn't work.

Tom played Jesse a song on his ukulele.

That didn't work.

Tom did his super-duper jump dance—twice—but . . .

Jesse only blew bubbles.

"He might want a different food," suggested
Tom's mother. Tom tried fresh fish flakes. He tried

fish kibbles, fish chips, and even fancy fish fries.
Jesse ate everything and stayed upside down.

"He's lonely. He needs another fish," said Monty
from next door.

The next day Tom brought Flo home from the fish store.

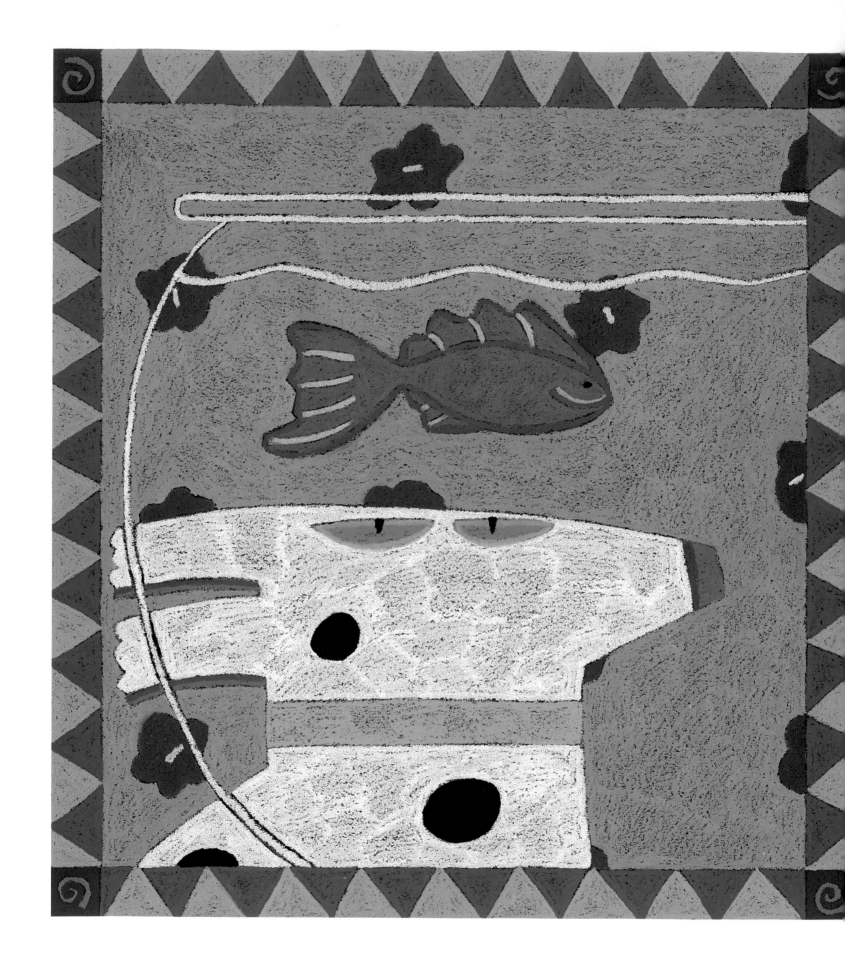

Flo swam around happily—right side up.

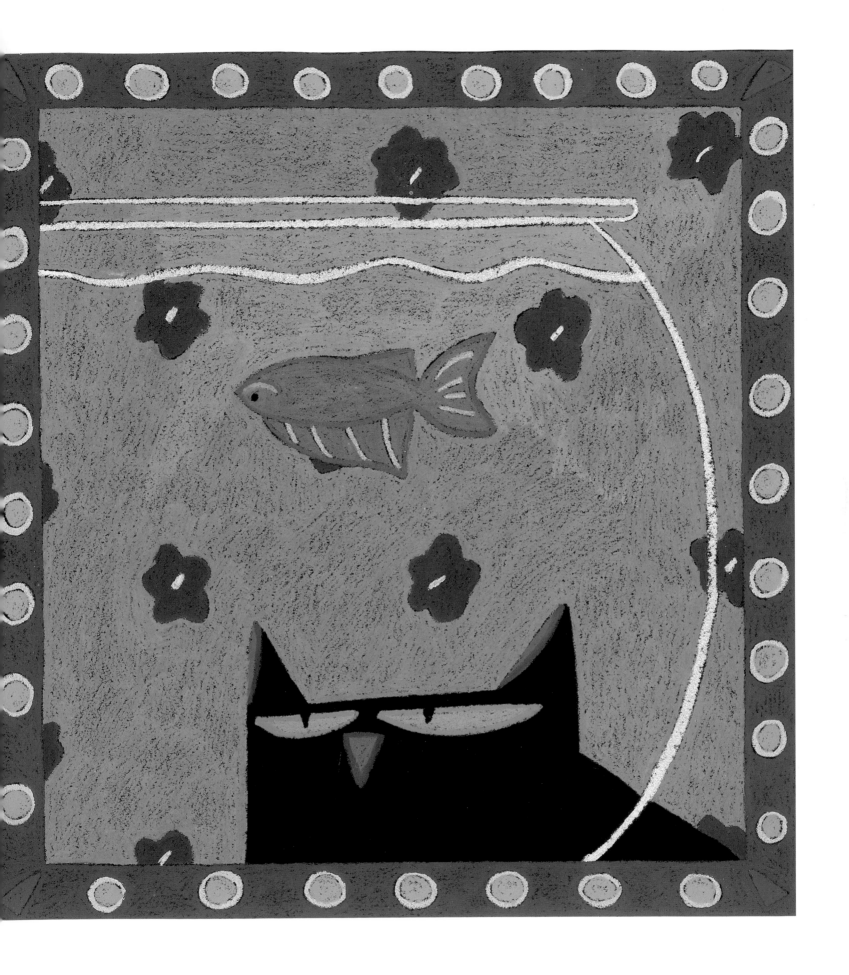

Jesse swam around happily—upside down.

Tom looked at his fish. Jesse didn't look bored or
hungry or lonely or anything but upside down.

Tom had an idea.

He did his best trick. He stood on his head. Now Jesse
looked right side up. Whenever Tom wanted to see Jesse